This Winnie-the-Pooh
book belongs to:

....

EGMONT

We bring stories to life

First published in Great Britain 2014
by Egmont UK Limited
The Yellow Building, 1 Nicholas Road
London W11 4AN
www.egmont.co.uk

Illustrated by Andrew Grey
Based on the 'Winnie-the-Pooh' works by A.A.Milne and E.H.Shepard
Illustrations © Disney Enterprises Inc. 2011

ISBN 978 1 4052 7297 1

Egmont is passionate about helping to preserve the world's remaining ancient forests.
We only use paper from legal and sustainable forest sources.

This book is made from paper certified by the Forest Stewardship Council® (FSC),
an organisation dedicated to promoting responsible management of forest resources.
For more information on the FSC, please visit www.fsc.org. To learn more about
Egmont's sustainable paper policy, please visit www.egmont.co.uk/ethical.

Winnie-the-Pooh
Pooh's Christmas Party

EGMONT

It was Christmas Eve, and Pooh was very excited. "Only one more day until Christmas!" he said.

Then, suddenly, Pooh remembered something *very* important.

"Oh bother!" he cried. "I forgot to send the invitations to my Christmas party!"

Pooh trudged through the snow to visit his friend Christopher Robin.

Christopher Robin opened his door, and Pooh said, "I've come to invite you to my Christmas party."

"But, Pooh, this says your party is *tonight*!" said Christopher Robin. "Is everything ready?"

"I might need a little help," Pooh admitted.

"Let's start by delivering these invitations!" Christopher Robin replied.

Pooh's friends were very excited to be invited to a Christmas party.

When they heard that Pooh needed help getting ready, they all volunteered.

It wasn't long before everyone was warming up inside Pooh's house.

"First, we should make a list of the things we need," Christopher Robin explained.

Everyone began calling out things at once:
"A Christmas tree!" "Biscuits!" "Decorations!"
"Stockings!" "Presents!"

Pooh could hardly write fast enough.

"Why don't we split into groups?" Christopher Robin said. "That way we can get more done!"

P ooh, Christopher Robin, and Piglet found
the perfect Christmas tree.

Kanga, Roo, and Tigger
made Christmas biscuits.

And Owl, Rabbit, and Eeyore
decorated Pooh's house.
Pooh and his friends worked very
hard all day.

"Let's start the party!" Pooh said. "Shall we sing some Christmas carols?"

"I'm too tired to sing," Piglet yawned.

"How about a game?" Pooh suggested. "Or some biscuits?"

"I believe we wore ourselves out preparing for the party!" said Rabbit.

Then Pooh had an idea.

He went into the kitchen and came back with a tray of steaming mugs.

"What's this?" Christopher Robin asked.

"Tea with extra honey and condensed milk," Pooh said. "It always makes me feel better."

"I don't think we'll need all those mugs," Christopher Robin whispered.

That's when Pooh looked around.

His friends were fast asleep.

"**B**ut we didn't even open the presents!" said Pooh.

"Silly old Bear," Christopher Robin said. "Spending time with friends is the best present of all."

The End.

Enjoy other wintery tales
with Winnie-the-Pooh and friends!

ISBN 978 1 4052 5775 6

ISBN 978 1 4052 6748 9

ISBN 978 1 4052 6282 8